For Cab and Katen
And especially for Mom

www.mascotbooks.com

A House for Wren

For more information, please contact:
Mascot Books
620 Herndon Parkway, Suite 320
Herndon, VA 20170
info@mascotbooks.com

Library of Congress Control Number: 2020903969

CPSIA Code: 978-1-64543-120-6
ISBN-13: PRT0620A

Printed in the United States

A HOUSE for Wren

Julie Beever

Illustrated by Diana Delosh

One fine spring morning, Mrs. Wren said to her husband, "Wren, dear, it's time to find a house. We are going to have a family!"

Wren was so thrilled he nearly fell off his perch. How wonderful! He quickly called Ms. Green Jay, the local real estate agent, to set up a meeting. The next day, Wren and Mrs. Wren flew to meet with her.

$\mathcal{M}$s. Green Jay greeted the Wrens warmly. "Welcome, welcome! It's so nice to meet you. You certainly came to the right place. Tell me a little about what you are looking for."

"Well," said Wren, "we would like a house that's sturdy and one that will feel safe, because we have a family on the way. We would also like to be near the water."

Treetop

"I would like it to have a nice view and, you know, be comfy. Oh, and I love flowers, too," said Mrs. Wren. "It would be nice to live near a garden."

"I'm just sure we can find the perfect house for you. However, this time of year we have a lot of interest in our homes, it being spring and all. Let me look around and find out what is available," said Ms. Green Jay. "We can go house hunting tomorrow."

Café

The next morning, the Wrens met Ms. Green Jay in a flowering bush at the edge of the woods.

Ms. Green Jay pointed to a cozy home nestled in the crook of a branch. "The first place I'm going to show you is this darling little cottage. It is very well built by one of our most popular contractors, Hummingbird, who works very quickly.

"It is constructed of twigs, plant fibers, leaves, and is held together with spider silk. Hmm . . . It seems there is a lot of interest in the tiny house right now."

"It is quaint," said Mrs. Wren, "but truly too small for us."

"Right, right," said Ms. Green Jay. "I understand. On to the next home."

"This next home is lofty, with a bird's-eye view, if you know what I mean. It is rambling and very spacious. You would be located closer to town where there is so much to see and do! Great Kiskadee built this house a couple of years ago, and it just came on the market. The exterior is made of sticks, bark, grass, and moss, while the inside is lined with wool and feathers . . . very soft, yet strong. Take a look at it and let me know what you think," said Ms. Green Jay.

"Well, it certainly has a view," Wren sighed, "but, it is so high, I'm afraid we would worry about the children getting too close to the edge. It is just not what we are looking for."

"Let's keep looking, then. Lots to see, lots to see! On to the next home," Ms. Green Jay said.

"This next home has what we call an open floor plan," Ms. Green Jay explained as she pointed at a flimsy Dove nest made of a few twigs and stems loosely thrown together. "Does this fit your needs?" asked Ms. Green Jay.

"This one has possibilities,"
Wren chirped excitedly.

"Dear, it's just not quite
right. It lacks something.
It doesn't seem very sturdy,"
said Mrs. Wren sadly.

"*N*ot to worry," comforted Ms. Green Jay. "We have several more really nice homes in the neighborhood. Here, take a look at this one! This sturdy nest was built by one of our premier homebuilders, Mrs. Oriole, who wove it herself out of fibers and twine. Why, it is so strong, it withstood a category F2 tornado several years ago."

"It is very beautiful and obviously safe. But, there's not much of a view," said Wren.

"No problem. On to the next home," Ms. Green Jay said.

"*R*ight over here is one of our most unique homes," Ms. Green Jay twittered excitedly.

"It was painstakingly carved into this oak tree many years ago.

"Oops! We are a little too late! It looks like my colleague, Mr. Cardinal, has just sold this home to Mr. Woodpecker. On to the next home!"

"*N*ow, for this next showing, I have just one thing to say: Location, location, location!" cooed Ms. Green Jay. "This area is prime real estate. It even has a water feature! This lovely stream flows right through the property. You could live at the water's edge. It doesn't get any better than that! What do you think?"

"Where is the house?" Wren and Mrs. Wren asked, looking this way and that.

"That's the beauty of it! You get to build your own home. Make it exactly like you want! It can be perfect!" exclaimed Ms. Green Jay.

"Oh, I don't know. I don't think we are ready to build a house ourselves, yet. This will be our first home. I believe we need one that is already built," stammered Wren.

"Very well," said Ms. Green Jay, getting a little nervous. "I have one last idea."

𝓜s. Green Jay hopped through the grass, leading Wren and Mrs. Wren to the next property. "I don't know if I should even mention it. A new house has come on the market, and it's just around the corner. I understand it was built by some new contractors, and I'm not at all familiar with their work. However," Ms. Green Jay said as she got a better look at the house, "they show great promise!"

"*T*hat's it!" exclaimed Wren and his wife as they spotted the colorful new birdhouse hanging from a strong, sturdy limb. "That is exactly what we are looking for! We'll take it!"

"It is just lovely," cried Ms. Green Jay. "Truly one of a kind! Amazing floor plan! Why, there's even an above-ground swimming pool nearby! And look at all of those restaurants!"

"And flowers," sighed Mrs. Wren.
"Look at all of the beautiful flowers!"

*S*ome time later . . .

From his perch atop the roof of their new birdhouse, Wren watched his family flying and playing about in their new neighborhood. He looked down at his new home and smiled. He was happy. It was the perfect house for Wren.

House Wren Fact Sheet

Description: The House Wren is a small, brown, energetic bird with a big, colorful, trilling voice. It may be found flitting around backyards or wooded areas.

Diet: The House Wren's diet consists mostly of insects and spiders.

Nest: The House Wren's nest is comprised of a soft cup lined with grass, feathers, and a variety of other material placed on a twiggy base. While the House Wren will build this nest inside natural crevices, bird houses, or woodpecker holes, it has been known to creatively build nests under the hoods of parked cars, in discarded shoes, in the top of a pipe, or in the pocket of an old shirt draped over the yard fence.

Young: The House Wren lays approximately five to eight small, spotted eggs. The incubation period is approximately two weeks. Once hatched, both male and female parents feed the young. Two weeks or so after hatching, the young birds leave the nest.

Julie Beever taught elementary reading to struggling readers for over twenty years. Her own love of reading began at an early age when her mother made up stories and rhymes to keep her young children amused. Julie divides her time between the South Texas brush country of Pearsall and the Texas hill country of Concan, where she enjoys photography, birding, and writing.